STORIES OF CREATION
AND DESTRUCTION

Stories of Creation and Destruction

Poems and Musings

by

MONICA TIMBAL

Adelaide Books
New York / Lisbon
2019

STORIES OF CREATION AND DESTRUCTION
Poems and Musings
By Monica Timbal

Copyright © by Monica Timbal

Cover design © 2019 Adelaide Books

Illustrations by Pixabay under Creative Commons CC0

Published by Adelaide Books, New York / Lisbon
adelaidebooks.org

Editor-in-Chief
Stevan V. Nikolic

For any information, please address Adelaide Books
at info@adelaidebooks.org

or write to:

Adelaide Books
244 Fifth Ave. Suite D27
New York, NY, 10001

ISBN: 978-1-951896-01-0
Printed in the United States of America

This is a work of fiction. Names, characters, places and incidents are either the product of the author's imagination or have been used fictitiously. Any resemblance to actual persons, living or dead, establishments, locations or events is entirely coincidental.

Acknowledgement

With deep gratitude to Riccardo, my partner in everything. This work is the result of his endless patience and assistance.

whatever is destroyed

is built again

in different shape or form

we are always born

of remnant thoughts,

of lingering desires,

forged anew in cosmic fire.

Life is a progressive, outward movement. It develops like a flower blossom. From the bud, we can never imagine its mature stage. In death, we go inwards. Movement ceases. A time of rest and assimilation.

I am that space where
life goes forth her myriad motions
and death recedes with quiet devotion.

Our origins are shrouded in mystery. Only deep silence allows the mind to penetrate behind the movement and the noise of the world. Here, we may get a glimpse of our infinite existence.

that forbidden sphere

no human gaze can peer

but only speculate

about our birthplace,

lingering silence opened

a window into space

when I came to see

that never was I not,

and never will I not be.

When we awake to the realization that the events in our lives reflect our minds, the world becomes a mirror for our growth. We are no longer separate. We no longer blame others or depend on others. Instead, we take responsibility for what happens to us. This is how we become truly free.

there is no one outside
to blame or to fight
the world is within you
each person, each event
a facet of your self
that yet remains to be embraced.
go deeper than the surface
recognize the voice that whispers
"Wake up! Wake up!"

Silence is fulfilling, rich and full of wisdom. Let the world go on with its activity. It is in moments of silence and doing nothing that we withdraw into eternal time.

the soul holds stories of eternity

which it shares in moments of tranquility.

It is very easy to get entangled in life's dramas, and forget what we truly are. While the mind likes complications, the spirit loves simplicity.

time after time

I fail to realize

my true path in life

and lose my ways

in a mind-built maze.

Peace is full acceptance of things as they are right now. There are endless desires in the world, but when we are satisfied in the present moment, we already have all there is to have.

to the heart at peace

life returns with many gifts

but it stays fulfilled

in the emptiness of things.

What can the outside world offer us that we don't already hold within? Looking outward for fulfillment always ends in disappointment. At some point, we discover our own source of inner joy, peace and love. It has always been there.

in vain we seek relentlessly

some inner hunger to fulfill

hollow, like a sea shell

forgetting that the music

has always played within.

We are asleep, thinking we are separate and alone, feeling that the world is an adversary, working against us. Awakening is recognizing our larger self, our connectedness to everything. It is recognizing we play a hand in creating our own reality.

sleeper, awaken!

your dream is dissolving,

a new face evolving

to cosmic life you now belong

the One reality is now your song.

Is life happening 'to' us, or are we more deeply involved in its unfolding? The real purpose of life is about remembering our origins, awakening to our forgotten, divine consciousness and to the reality that we are.

let's play gods
and build a world
in our very likeness
a phantom dream! with wicked plots
and unlikely circumstances.
then let's forget
and pretend we are
Mortals in the game.

The world is noisy and full of distractions. It pulls us in many directions. How can we expect to discover the vastness of who we really are, when we are always on the run? We need to pause, keep quiet, and listen to the voice within...

sailor on a sea of turbulence

I meet my real self

on the crest of silence.

Man has many stories of creation, enough to keep mind busy for lifetimes. The truth only starts revealing itself when we take the journey inwards, to our silent core. "Random thoughts, unwanted feelings and emotions".

forgive my mind!
it tries to find its comfort
in man-made fairy tales
to wrap itself
and keep amused
sheltered from the truth
behind deterring veils.

A certain detachment from the events of life is healthy. It gives us a better perspective on what really matters, and life becomes more enjoyable. Being detached, we drop the heavy burdens that hold us down. The mind becomes free, light and focused.

detached. around me

a garden of delight!

no worldly hankers

hold me down.

my sight, on a goal divine

my guide, a buddha-like mind.

Nothing remains the same in this world; change is the only constant. Why cling to that which will change and often leads to suffering? That which is aware, is unchanging. Staying fixed in the awareness of change, nothing can disturb our essence.

no changing form

will capture my soul

I will travel the road

with the changeless beyond.

To the novice, reincarnation can appear pointless—
endless cycles of life and death—a trap from which it is
impossible to escape. From this standpoint life appears
as a burden rather than an opportunity for liberation.

cast into world affairs

I don't remember wishing to go there!

to play the game of birth and death

trapped in all that strife and fight

without escape in sight!

When the forces of above meet the forces of below, when consciousness enters matter, when the Sky meets the Earth duality seeks to re-unite into the one source.

she's all dressed up,

lacy mists cover her gaze

promises of oceanic depths

her bosom full in mountain peaks,

rivers rushing through her veins

and volcanic, youthful folly

gushing

in anticipation for her lover, the Sky

he opens his arms

with great expectation

in birth of a new creation.

Nothing in the world is good or bad in itself, but mind will categorize and label things as such. What seems good today might be bad tomorrow; what helps one person may hinder another. Terrible problems can harbour grace. Such qualities are subtle and fluid, and drawing borders between them can obscure the greater vision of the whole. It is better not to invest too much attachment to such differentiations, as they might change at any moment. Life flows whether we divide or not.

the distance between good and bad

in mind alone is born

and builds a mind-made hell

of the rose's thorns.

Life is a great mystery. The moment we feel we found our answer, its changes into something else. Like children enjoying their games, we too can adopt a playful, light- hearted attitude to decipher its mysteries.

searching for answers

to this cosmic puzzle

riddled in games

like childhood charades.

The silent mind, like the Buddha mind, is like an empty sky free of clouds of unnecessary thoughts. Such inner clarity and stillness make a person grounded and focused. To such a person, anything is achievable. The world is at their feet.

silent buddha, rooted in your stillness,

your mind, like empty, cloudless skies

no thought can enter

yet the whole world abides.

Such is the paradox of life: we are the creators, and at the same time, we are merely passing by. This helps us understand why the world sometimes does not feel like our original home. We are gatherers of experiences, and after we learn our lessons, we move on…

we don't truly belong

we only color the world

on a canvass of emptiness

with the music of our laughter

the pain of our tears

aspirations and high hopes

a dance of passing shadows yet

our human 'tour de force'.

Our skin marks the boundaries of our physical body. But our full existence extends much further than that. As the heart opens, we find an ocean of love waiting for us.

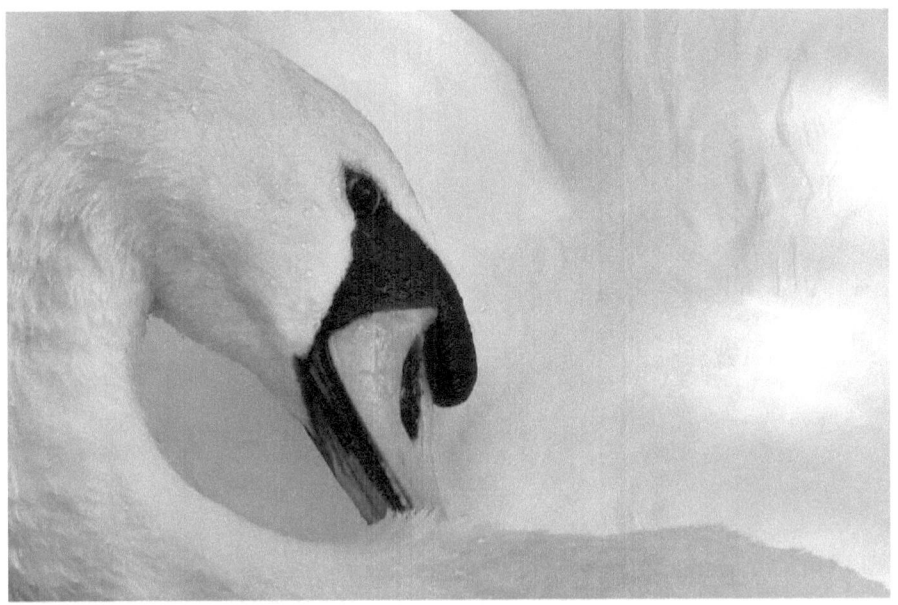

my boundaries melting

in effulgent glow

no longer the body I know

a new heart opens above

accepting

cosmic waves of generous love.

How priceless are those moments of inspiration
that give birth to our creative works? They raise
our spirit above the ordinary life. If we could only
catch them and keep them closed in a jar...

waves of inspiration arrive

leaving gifts

of rare elation.

The mind does not have the will or the spiritual forces that the heart contains. When we rely on the mind only to accomplish our soulful yearnings, chances are we will not get very far. But when we lead with the heart, nothing is impossible, because the heart is rooted in oneness. The heart is its own source of inspiration.

demand less, my body is weak

it will not keep up

a slave to its own cravings.

give heart the lead

it knows no boundaries

and is world-embracing.

Meditation creates a distance between our thoughts and our true self. Our life starts to appear like a movie that we are watching, rather than participating in. How many such movies have we watched? How many different faces have we worn?

watching moving pictures
of my fleeting life
"I knew this face once"!
that person gone
and many other masks I wore
with both shame and pride.
now far removed from all the show
a silent watcher
free and unconcerned.

The deeper we go within, the more we see that the outside world reflects our inner state. There is no separation. Recognizing this, we start taking responsibility for our thoughts. Then, we take the position of creators and can design the life we want.

to find the roots of our thoughts

is to find the source of our world

and regain the power

to manifest and transform.

Creation manifests itself in infinite variety of different forms! That is its magnificence and splendor. But don't get confused by forms; learn to see beyond to the One source that brings everything into existence.

we are entangled in forms.

so many sounds and scents and lovely shapes

to keep us entertained in this game

of hide and seek!

playing with our very selves,

unable to see our face

a skewed reflection

in the cosmic perfection.

Love can be cleansing, recharging and renewing. It can offer an opportunity to dive deeper into ourselves, and to discover parts we were unaware of. Ultimately, our search for love is a search for our deepest self.

let me be your cleansing sea,
fervently embracing waves
with sorrow devouring depths
and gentle rocking sway.

Awakening is seeing life as the mirror of our selves: a series of events that are meant to guide us towards a higher understanding. Nothing happens without reason and we can learn from any moment in our lives. What appears to be a painful event, can be a door to inner transformation. We just need to be open.

every barrier, hurdle, and every obstacle

there

by the universe undertaken

to shake and to awaken.

The Hindus consider the OM to be the original sound of creation. Everything in the universe vibrates, creating movement and giving rise to forms. When the mind is very still, it is possible to hear this mystical sound that gives birth to all there is.

at last, the silence broken

by simplest sound, the OM

releasing its vibration

and creating worlds—

reflections of a higher maker.

dive deep in soul to hear

divine music of the cosmic spheres!

Out of one essence, everything arises. We experience the world in a myriad of forms, but they all have the same root. Knowing this, we are no longer confused by difference and variety. We can be stable and undisturbed in the all-abiding formlessness which is the mother of all forms.

grab me with arms of wisdom,

World Without Forms,

hold me in your silence

nourishing my soul.

We are the stories, we are the creators and we are always in the process of creating. In this world ruled by impermanence, how real are our creations? Could it all be a dream?

all man's glorious stories

written in ghost ink,

dreaming of leaving his footprints

on the warp of time.

but would he know,

he has been here before?

before time was even born?

We always seek outwards, expecting the world to give us the answers to all our questions. All the world does, however, is remind us of what we truly are: reality itself.

looking out into the world
wondering where we belong
but the world points back
"You are that! You are that!"

We constantly weave around us mental butterflies
that reflect our intentions. With love, we
create the most beautiful reality.

laying a carpet of stars

to light your way back

to my longing heart.

When an unconscious behaviour is brought forth
and recognized, it is illumined and transformed. An
awakened mind shines in its own knowingness. It
is truly like a sun illumining its own path.

of water born,

impelled by waves and tides

and fluxes

by celestial planets conducted,

our silent mother, Moon,

guiding from dark shadows

of unconscious mind—Pandora's box!

step out into the light

be illumined by the Sun

an awakened mind

is its own compass on the ocean of life.

Humans have unimaginable powers. Like gods, we have the potential to create with thought alone. It is our negativity, desires and habits that prevent us from discovering our divine powers. Ironically these same barriers destroy the spontaneous pleasure that comes from just enjoying what we have.

we are unwitting makers

building splendid worlds

on the echoes of our thoughts

and destroying our delight

with the grasping of our wanting.

Everything occurs in cycles; the universe itself is formed and destroyed in cosmic cycles, called 'yugas' in Sanskrit. While Shiva dances, life unfolds. When he stamps his foot down, watch out! The destruction of a cycle is near.

worlds are built and worlds destroyed

by gods contented or annoyed.

entire universes crumbling

at Shiva's mere foot stomping.

We are alchemists at life, continually transforming our nature
into something finer. We need to dig down through layers
of untruths to find the golden core—our purest being.

forged in earth, water and fire

the elements of our attire,

we pierce unceasingly inside,

unfooled by matter or demise,

alchemists of life,

to uncover the golden core

and transmute our ignoble nature

into auric abode.

Inspiration can come like unexpected thunder, filling us with a rush of excitement followed by joy. But it is so fleeting! Melting quicky away, it leaves us longing for more.

moments of inspiration,

like ice flowers on a window

patterns of elation.

Travelling on the wheel of life and rebirth, we go deeper and deeper into the mysteries of existence. Birth itself is an appearance in form only, and death is never truly an end.

with mind blank,

another baby crying,

appearing to be born but never dying,

a soul

picking up where it left behind

a trace

from time immemorial.

The mind is analytical and is often caught in its logical webs. In its analysis, it separates reality into parts. Only the heart has the ability to see the whole. In its identification with the world around us, it has the mystical ability to go beyond what is merely visible to the physical eye and logical mind. It is through the heart that the doors to eternity are opened.

my body tells me stories of mortality
my heart whispers truths of eternity.

Nature is a source of endless variety. But like the lotus flower whose petals are each different and unique, everything in creation manifests from, and is sustained by, a single root. The essence is one.

the lotus flower opens

in a sky salute

manifold of splendid petals

and so hiding

One single root.

Nothing we build can withstand the passage of time. Maybe time is teaching us not to cling to anything, but rather to enjoy the moment. When we truly live in the continuous moment, we live in eternity.

the waves of time are harsh

and ruthlessly erase

all the sand castles of our lives.

There is no beginning without ending, no birth without death. Between these two shores, life continuously unfolds. When we accept this endless cycle, we stop favoring one over the other, and see them as equal.

with every end a new beginning

carves its face,

ethereal flowers on the memory trace,

new stories of creation and destruction

our lasting embrace

with our divine seduction.

We are conditioned by society to feel we need a partner to be happy. We are always looking out there for love. But our greatest treasure is within our very selves. When we discover this, we become whole individuals. Ironically, we also become better partners to each other.

remind me of the love I've lost

looking for another

deeming the world a stranger

waiting to fill my cup

ignoring my inner,

dormant treasure.

Nothing lies outside us; we are pure awareness that encompasses both life and death. In life, we move, in death we rest. We are the source.

within me

both life and death are born

two unlikely sisters

displaying many forms

of endings and beginnings.

such mesmerising whirl!

making me forget

I am the source of all.

Desire ultimately fills us with anxiety and disappointment. It distracts us from fully enjoying the present moment. How much lighter we are when we accept whatever is being offered, without endlessly craving other things!

I tip-toe through life
with carefree attire
leaving only a song
unspoiled by desire.

Walking through life, we sometimes encounter deja vu and synchronicity. We get the feeling that we've been here before, maybe even walked this same path. Is it possible that we are repeating old patterns to learn new lessons?

a soundless music calls my soul

into a world unknown

unearthing traces, I implore,

have I walked this path before?

Looking for god is like a shadow looking for its shadow maker; always side by side yet never quite meeting. There is no need to find what we have never lost, what we are looking for is within our very nature.

in dreams we meet

the gods that made us

and birthed the world below

like a shadow

following its maker

we try to catch the face

of our original creator.

Lost in the routine of daily activities, there is little opportunity for heroism. But we all have a hero inside, and it is up to us to unveil it.

my heart is brave, I am convinced,

it just remains to be revealed

underneath my daily deeds.

this ordinary mundane life

leaves little chance to unmask

my inner warrior, my inner Joan of Arc.

We all have life events in which we felt we were defeated or in which we lost control. In quiet reflection however, these events can frame a greater whole—one in which we realize that everything happened the way it had to happen. Control is an illusion. Life has a flow of its own; the less we fight it, the easier we flow with it.

we are re-arranging pawns
on the chess game of life,
carefully planning our moves
in patterns already designed.

The physical body may die, but the spirit is rooted in the infinite and is undying. It has unlimited potential and is untouched by the death of the physical body. Get in touch with it, learn to listen to its song.

my body is weak and can't keep up

with soul's unerring drive.

it stumbles and suffers

over endless desires

thus enticing death—

our greatest liar!

envision that this soul's light

will conquer the mind,

condemning death to die!

Meditation brings the realization that our innermost thoughts, habits and tendencies, ultimately create our reality. If we live life unconsciously, we lose sight of our true potential and can fall victim to our own careless thoughts. But this realization brings a new awareness; we start paying attention to the kind of thoughts we nurture, and to the thoughts we want to pluck before they grow roots.

dive deep into the silence of your soul
and catch the shadows of your thoughts
before they surface
and manifest your world.

The cosmic game of life and death goes on eternally. Our present life is our dream to enjoy, to suffer through and change. We can do anything but willingly attempt to stop it.

you can dance, or crawl, or fall,

or take your exit, if you can.

our place assured, there are no rules

anything will go in the Cosmic Plot.

but avoid at all cost

to make

the gravest mistake of all,

and attempt to stop the game.

What a wonderful, mystical moment when the sun comes up each morning, and floods the earth with light!

earth awaits her day

in new expectation each dawn

like a lover stealing

golden kisses from the sun.

When we cling to a memory, hoping to beautify our present, we cannot be fully in the present. Every moment brings a new awareness, there is no need to carry on the dead past. No matter how beautiful, a withered rose has no scent to share.

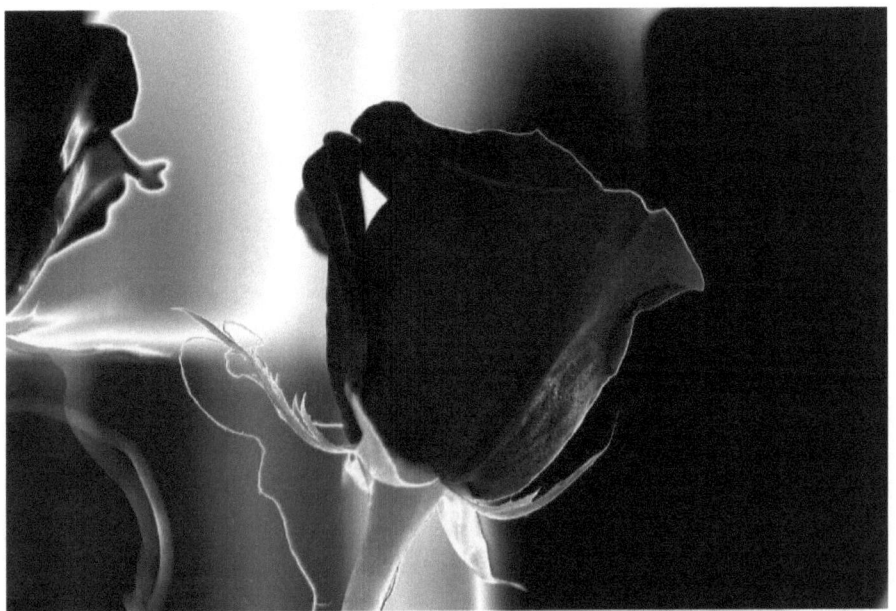

like withered roses

adorning my nightstand

I'm chasing memories

for a vanished scent.

A baby sees the world afresh and without attachment.
Many spiritual practices aim to arrive at the same pure state.

we must leave as we arrived,

naked and unspoiled,

empty in the mind,

selfless and desireless

in the world for one goal.

for what is soul

if not a mere visitor

of this fleeting world?

'Neti, neti' is a Sanskrit expression meaning 'not this, not that'. It is used as a meditation method to negate identification with all things which we are not, until we arrive at the truth that we are—the authentic Self.

deceived by forms, and skin and bones

on an eternal search for truth

neti, neti! not this, not that,

nothing that can be pointed at,

for it cannot be seen and need remain unsaid.

a truth so well disguised

by the fabric of our mind

and concealing the final wonders

that we are our own designers.

Through the silence of our soul we get glimpses into dimensions that otherwise remain hidden: the mystery of our existence. But who is really looking?

windows into a soul

that gazes into unknown

worshiper of love affairs

has anybody lived there?

In our society, death has a bad reputation. It is the last unspoken taboo. It scares us, it is unfamiliar and unknown. But life and death are partners; we could not know one without the other. In all things, after movement, there comes a period of rest. Thus balance is maintained.

I'll uncover your truth, death,

your deceiving demeanor

pretending you're the reaper

filling all with fear.

All life is soul's dreaming. Whether is it marked by love or suffering, it is all part of the dream. When we awaken, we begin to see through its ephemeral nature.

one thousand lives

one thousand deaths

dreams of luscious love

and dreams of painful loss

mark the shores of memory

on my river of reverie.

We recognize angels by the light they emanate, filled with purity, goodness, abundance of spirit. We all have that light within.

treading so light

in the company of angels,

she's seen from above

by the dazzle in her crown.

The body is full of desires, harnessing our senses and dictating the course of our energy. But we forget that we have will—the power to examine our desires and to decide which to follow, and which to ignore.

in a world of my own creation

I foolishly fall victim

to my body's temptations

filling me with needs!

mistaking the creator

for the player

'I bear the outcome of all my deeds.

The inner light of Self must be acknowledged and embraced before it can start shining through us and into the world. Living occurs on a higher frequency, marking the end of fear, anxiety, and doubt. We are glorious again, as we were always meant to be. The time has come.

timeless child

this is your time to shine

your glory face

your endless grace

creating worlds

like open skies

without disguise

of forms and names.

The spiritual path is paradoxical; the more we grasp, the further the goal seems to move. Eternity shows its face unexpectedly, when we stop looking for it.

eternity's hidden endowments

discovered

in droplets of melting moments.

Life demands a lot from us, from our bodies.
After a long life of activity and effort, death is a
welcome relief. It feels good to stop and not be
involved in the whirlpool of life for a while.

I'm tired still.

this body craves some rest

from all this life has brought

and all the fights I fought.

let me lie down

please, cover me now

in your welcomed death cloak.

Love is one of life's most enjoyable experiences. It fills us with sweetness, and it raises us above the ordinary.

lover's kisses

early dewdrops

make my morning blisses.

Our busy lives leave no space for us to truly know ourselves. Pure being arises in precious moments of doing nothing, of quiet mind, of undisturbed attention. Then we create an opening for our soul to make itself known.

in moments of empty meaning
we find the fullness of our being.

The whole of creation is imbued with spirit. Why be restricted to one place of worship to lend your heart in devotion? We can train our vision to see spirit everywhere, at all times, and live constantly in its splendor.

don't go searching

in temples and churches!

spirit doesn't only dwell in there.

why look to a monk in robes?

spirit flows freely everywhere

in every action, in every motion,

it weaves the fabric of creation.

look, see, embrace it!

it is our source, our destination.

No words or sounds can possibly transcribe
the experience or meaning of being alive. Only
silence can inspire in us the mystery of all.

the world speaks to me

not in words or sounds

but in silences profound.

The mind, by its nature, divides and separates. It takes in information and tries to analyze and categorize the world. The heart, on the hand, goes forth and identifies with the world. Its understanding is mystical and it transcends the limited capabilities of the mind. Only heart can feel the oneness of existence.

heart holds secrets

that mind cannot recognize

and therefore denies.

The secrets of love include an intoxicating power that keeps it lingering around us, leaving an indelible stamp and a lasting impression.

each whispered kiss

prolonged and kept

in secret shadows on my lips.

We can only ignore the callings of our soul for so long. When we take the dive within, we are embarking on the eternal journey to our most authentic self.

two thousand lives I have ignored

the callings of my soul,

its whispers in my dreams

and heralds from beyond,

enticing me to follow

the pathless path of inner worlds,

wishing to show me

realms of the beginnings,

my birthplace, my original face.

The Buddha said that all suffering is due to man's ignorance of his true nature. In our largest self, we are eternal consciousness, unlimited and undying. Not knowing this leaves us victims of a life that appears to work against us.

we cry

unsuspecting of our grandeur

we crawl

unaware we can fly

we suffer

ignorant of our power,

forgetting we are undying and unbound.

In the eternal unfolding of consciousness, both birth and death are comings and goings. We must look beyond, to find that which is ever unchanging. The journey into that quest begins with our self-discovery.

not birth, nor death

carry the answers to my quest.

they play a momentary note

in an endless cosmic song.

Science has established that matter is mostly empty space. Then what is it that makes the world appear dense? Could it be that at the root of all manifestation we discover consciousness itself? "The whole world is beginning to look like a great thought" said British physicist James Jeans in 1930.

out of thought

the world emerged

from subtlest of substance,

a sleeping god

immersed in dreams

of infinite enchantment,

dreams of love and war and loss

that man has called his own

and lays as stepping stones

to pave his way back home.

One of the major realizations we can have in life is that we are creators of our reality. Our happiness is in our hands. We reap the fruits of our thoughts.

untroubled at last!

life has given me a break

and now I have the upper hand.

I'll mold her and transform her

and make her my friend

"Life, you are cruel,

but I am wiser!"

As long as we don't know our true place within the world, we feel like strangers. But life is a continuous dance between our thoughts and our manifested reality. As we uncover the power of our thoughts, we start living our divine relation with everything.

you a stranger no longer, my world,

your secrets uncovered

in the roots of my thoughts

my longing, my goal

whose embrace I always sought.

I dance with your glance!

Awakening to truth can make us lose our minds,
turning upside down everything we believed
about the world. Thus detached, we remain in
the world, but are no longer *of* the world.

I'm so divinely crazy!

World, your rules don't apply to me!

I dance with you, I play your song,

but I don't truly belong.

Each person is a universe, full of innumerable possibilities. With our choices we can build a life of splendor, or we can build a life of despair. Each choice we make plays a part in a grander cosmic outcome.

with every soul, a universe is born

bearing man's triumph

carrying man's fall.

at every moment we sew our destiny,

choosing filaments

for our cosmic tapestry.

We have much to learn from nature! It offers its beauty generously, yet asks for nothing in return. We too can accomplish our worldly duties without expectations. An act performed with full-hearted effort can be its own reward.

the lyre bird sings his song
and asks nothing in return.
man completes each occupation
expecting much ovation.

We can gain a deeper understanding of sound by first experiencing silence profound. Finding roots in silence, exterior noise or chaos will no longer disturb our inner calm.

the stone is silent.

in its muteness

it holds all answers.

if man can learn

to be like stone

all the wisdom

will be his own.

Doubt can only live in the mind. By its very nature, the heart is free of doubt. As mind becomes quieter, we make space for the heart to blossom and to come forth. We become more aware of the similarities between us rather than the differences. We open to universal love.

surrender

from a torrent of doubt

into an ocean of love.

my heart renders

a new face

a new dimension

opens in a world embrace.

Much of our suffering persists because we don't let it go. Every day is a fresh start. Every day we undergo a new birth. Today, I don't have to be who I was yesterday. We can start each day with a clean slate, and so keep the spontaneity of each moment alive.

each morning is a new reminder

that you

are the sole designer.

clean and empty we start like babes.

why carry again

yesterday's remains?

Heaven and hell are states of our own making. When love accompanies our actions, then life responds and we live in a state of harmony. When dissatisfaction and negativity is our nature, we live in a state of constant turmoil.

heavy stones pave my way to hell,

stones of hate, anger and deception

stones of separation.

heaven's ladder I build with deeds of love,

in patience, giving and acceptance

both I build with my own hands.

This world is made to awaken us to our true vastness. The world is not pre-determined, it is not an inanimate clockwork. It is organic, alive and leading us into deeper being, if we only pay attention.

open your eyes

this world is alive

with a heart of its own

that longs for your return

eyes bright as stars in the night

Sun's glow pours below

its golden love.

come home!

through your body, in your breath

all the wisdom flows.

you are creation that knows.

Blissful being is beyond conditions, time or space. As everything in the world comes and goes, so the physical body dies, but being continues on, untouched by the process of change.

who are we, beneath this skin?

shadows of a self unseen

untouched by time

unbound by space

a longing for return to bliss

and childlike sight,

days spent in soul's kiss

and wondrous delight.

In little instances of thought-free reverie, the mind dives
into the timeless and eternal, and finds its true home.

to feel eternity

in a moment's delight

catching the wing beat

of a bird in flight.

From an ordinary standpoint, we can never the see whole picture; our vision and understanding is limited by our personal point of view, born of our experiences. The higher we go, the more our perspective enlarges. The personal sense of 'me' diminishes and a universal vision emerges. Seen from here, love is the glue holding it all together.

look up.

up!

from high above

the world is woven in threads

of love.

It is called by many names: Self, Presence, Being, Source, Awareness, Unity, the Witness, God, the One. It is the source of everything and is most subtle and mysterious. It reveals its secrets to the sincerest seekers.

a breath finer than air

supports the whole creation

upholding life and death

on wings of sublime secrecy

and unnamed origins.

hidden

behind your seeing,

hidden

behind your being,

who told you that you were

born in life?

is not life

born through you?

carrying your thoughts

yet thought cannot reach

its profundity.

without it, nothing is or isn't.

outside the boundaries of time and space,

untouched and always unchanged

by moving pictures

in the game of human race.

the golden breath

the all-illumined Self.

Everything occurs in cyclical motions. Often, we have the feeling "I've been here before", because we move forward in a spiral fashion, revisiting similar circumstances, but encompassing deeper truths.

from time immemorial
we play again and again
the stories of creation
in infinite variation.
wearing new garments
we still remain dormant.

the stories are the same
only appearances change.

Awakening opens a new perspective: that of eternal existence, in which life occurs because we Are.

how could we know

we are undying

and are never born

when out of mothers we seem

to enter a world

foreign and cold,

appearing powerless,

fragile and small.

how could we guess

the world arises only

within our very self?

An open heart is both the doorway to fulfillment in the here and now, as well as a window into the hidden mysteries of life.

with heart open

light and carefree wisps of bliss

leave kisses on my lips

and whispers

of eternal wisdom.

Nothing man-made can compare with the riches within us. An expanded consciousness is unfathomable; the universe itself bows down to the Buddha.

I met a man of no possessions

more of a shadow than an earthly presence,

a passing trace,

yet an awareness so vast

that flowers bloom

where his foot has passed

and sun rays follow

his peaceful gaze.

It is painful to see beautiful things wither and die. Rather than holding on to beauty, hoping it might survive the ravages of time, instead love it, understand the essence of it, so that it will keep its beauty forever.

beauty aches in our inability

to maintain it

and leaves a lingering fragrance

on the hearts that knew it.

Only thoughts keep us back, often creating obstacles and fears out of nothing. They obscure our deeper potential, which is unlimited. "Whatever a monk keeps pursuing with his thinking and pondering, that becomes the inclination of his awareness" said the Buddha.

our fears cloud our vision
and cripple our capacity
for infinity.

From birth we are confined by limits placed on us by society. What if we refuse any limitation? What if we could erase everything we have been told we are, and rediscover ourselves? Would we find we have no limits?

they never told me
I could not be named
that my true face expressed
through every form
that my real body spread
in every corner
of this world and
beyond.
I had to find this
on my own
refusing labels
they gave me
of things that I was not.

In the physical world, we see separateness. In the ocean that is the ground of all consciousness, there are no individual drops. The ocean is One.

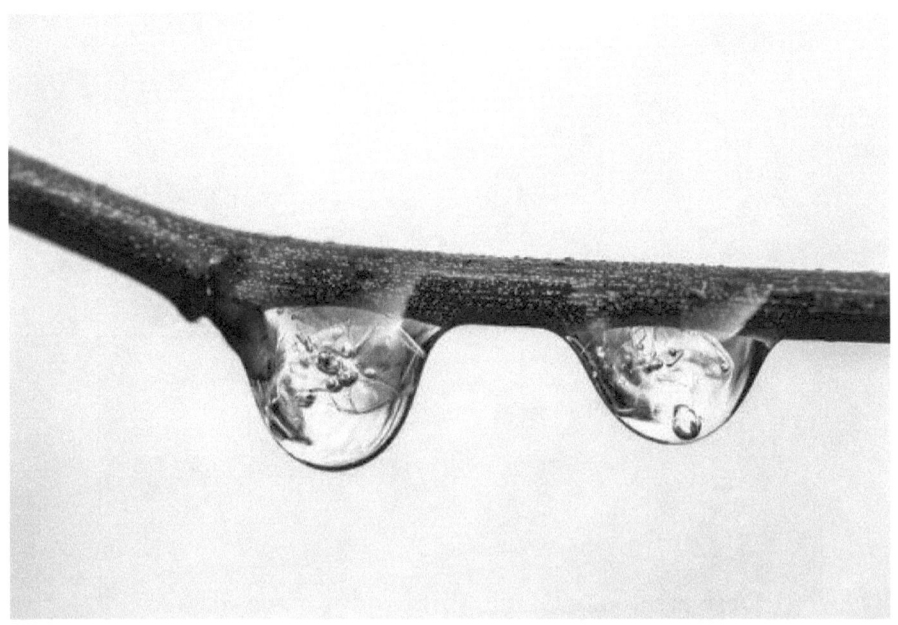

too many layers
still to break through.
truth is glorious
when it is naked
of 'I' or 'you'.

Deep meditation is still, silent and spacious like the bottom of an ocean. Personal identity dissolves, and only the truest essence, pure awareness, remains.

I fell asleep

into an ocean deep

of bluest peace

and boundless tranquility

forgetting my name

and with breath surrendered

all encompassing splendor

welcomed me

into my changeless home.

Pain and tribulation churn and purify the heart
making it gentler and more accepting. The heart is
a teacher and a path towards full realization.

with my heart

in a bud, like a flower

keeping my sight

on what I may become.

oh, Sun! your fire

has churned my painful past,

your light will blossom my

future at last.

All life is about going back to the source, to our truest being. It feels like a path we walk on, our life's stories, sufferings and glories. Eventually we realize all lives are dreams, and there is nowhere to arrive. We only need remember.

without a doubt

our river life flows

towards an ocean soul.

in arriving we recognize

we never left at all.

there is no coming nor going

in absolute being.

but what tales we've built;

"such stuff as dreams are made on."

bridges of love,

and prisons of despair!

Love does not always last as long as we hope, and it can leave painful scars on the heart. Instead of dwelling on the pain, what if we use it as fodder to grow something beautiful instead?

you walked across my naked soul

leaving footprints

where flowers now grow.

Consciousness is one, without separation. It encompasses everything and allows the dream that is life, to be. In this space, there is no you and me.

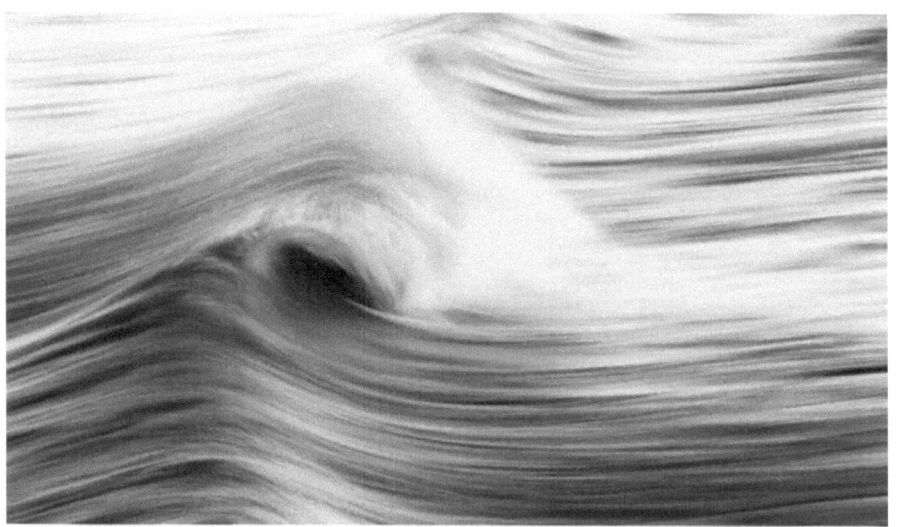

I drown my name

in the ocean of consciousness

and let the waves undo

any separation

between me and you.

Nothing we obtain from outside can fulfill us
for very long. Exterior satisfaction is temporary,
because the world is rooted in change. The greatest
treasures are eternal. They are found within.

looking for treasures

among earthly meager measures

man misses the pearl

hidden in his own soul.

The world is a stage for change and transformation. Death itself is transformation, one phenomenon passing into another. Nothing is ever lost.

death is another form of being

to the eye unseeing.

mere transitions.

hidden journeys.

day giving unto night.

winter changing into spring.

what death is there to grieve?

Because we identify with our physical bodies, we feel trapped by the constrictions of time. Meditation expands our boundaries beyond the body, so that we can experience a much larger self—the one that knows no death.

time grasps with iron chains

and keeps man a slave

in tales of illusion

of his body-cage.

Who is aware of all the comings and goings? Who is it that watches this changing show? Who implements the law of karma? The whole universe is awareness itself.

from silence it arises
echoes of our past devices
shaped in dreams
of man or woman
one life pauper, one life king
all results of our own deeds.
the universe is equanimous
to ruler or beggar
it only watches and returns
whatever each one earns,
a mere witness of this endless show
that is life and death.
since our origins, the timeless
toward our goal, the nameless.

Children live with spontaneity and full abandonment.
In that childlike, direct awareness, life feels
fulfilling and complete. We find bliss.

children's games and fervid glee

need nothing to achieve

and make life's dream complete

with self-abandoned bliss.

Sometimes we meet people and feel like we have always known them. If we perceive the unity of all, in essence, we are part of everyone, and everyone is part of us.

have we met this way before?

were you my lover, stealing kisses

or my brother, sharing childhood blisses.

maybe I met you

in my mother's sweet embrace.

who is to say? nothing is new.

what shape or form Self takes on

to entertain itself,

oh, this elusive cosmic game!

Cosmic vision is fluid. Boundaries are not so clear. In moments of highness, we can see our spirit everywhere.

the sun calls my name

rolling rays of golden flames

and lingering thought

like ocean waves caught

between the shores of now

and evermore.

Moments of spiritual insight are elusive, and impossible to describe. When they appear, we are filled with delight. But the moment we try to grasp them, they are already miles away.

sometimes we dance

this elusive partner

showing up at will and

filling me with thrills

of illumination…

seize her and she disappears.

Our true, original nature is spirit. It is simple and true. The human mind, the other hand, is complicated and capable of many games. It often prefers to hide behind lies rather than face the truth.

spirit wears the cloak of truth.

mind prefers ignorance, falsehood

and the folly of youth.

it fears the presence of the wise

where it might be disrobed

of its comforting lies.

We hold all the powers of the universe inside, and have yet to discover that. Many people put too much effort in chasing impermanent things, and not enough in nurturing the spiritual life.

we are mad!

kings of the world

acting as fools,

begging for crumbs

and wearing a blindfold

while holding inside

castles of gold.

The claws of materialism bind many of us. We gather
things hoping to bring meaning to our lives. Is
our spirit measured by the things the we own?

what are the colors of your soul?

have you glimpsed that which makes you whole?

why worship trinkets you gathered

along the road.

how will they help you

when your body turns cold?

Divine consciousness is everywhere, and when you move, you can feel the universe moving with you.

in words of wisdom

as vast as the seas

her whisper moving waves

through gentle breezes

and each breath sways

under fishermen's vessels

foamy peaks forming

at the linger of her fingertips.

How can we be sad, when we know ourselves to be eternal? How can we suffer, when we know ourselves to be the source of all there is? What can we need, when we already are everything? Only remember.

don't grieve, my child

for you were never born

and death cannot take you.

your body

does not contain you.

your mind

cannot define you.

you are the source of all.

within you, both space and time arise.

you are the eternal now—

the source of all existence.

you are the dream divine.

Time and space, thoughts and words, these are constructs which allow us to navigate this material world. They apply to the relative, but not to the absolute. When time and space dissolve, words are not necessary as no separation exists.

let us meet again
when we have no need
of names
in an ageless time
in a wordless space
I will know you
for your burning, inner blaze.
let us be at last
as rivers of devotion
merging
into the greater ocean
as we remember
we have never been apart.

Life has a flow of its own. Trying to control it leads to endless frustration. Letting go and learning to flow with life's flow brings peace and harmony. We create and follow our dreams, and finally let the universe take charge. Then we can be satisfied with any outcome.

veils are rising

I can see through the mist

loosening my grip

over life's order.

I am no longer life's commander.

I yield and surrender

to a gentler flow.

there is no more fear

the way ahead is clear.

we created and destroyed

again and again

unlikely authors

writers of legends

birthing new gods

while burying the old

builders of empires

and destroyers of nations

with much human love

with much human pathos

architects of order and of chaos.

who could fathom

a dance

of such magnificence?

Here in the west, we have placed the mind on a pedestal. We feel that an intelligent mind must be constantly busy, thinking, analyzing and weighing facts. But mind should be seen as a tool that serves us, not the other way around. When we are used by it, it becomes like a wild horse that takes us hither and yon. And ultimately, we lose our true connection to life and to being. The deepest truths are felt, not understood by the intellect.

be careful of those
who build a life
around their thoughts
and fiercely guard
their own self-made
prison.

Lucky is the person whose vision is so clear that they see the One essence behind all things. Just as the bottom of the ocean is unaffected by the changing waves at the surface, so a calm, abiding source consciousness gives rise to all experience. No matter how stormy the surface, the source remains calm, unchanged, untouched, and undying.

all that comes into being, will go out of being

and again, return into being

in another shape or form.

such is the nature of this world

and of phenomena.

so don't grieve or mourn

but know this eternal truth

find yourself as the one source

and give your love to all.

Our true essence, consciousness, has no dimension, it is timeless and outside space. In fact, time and space come out of it. It is closer to you than your own breath, more intimate than your own thoughts. In fact, it carries your breath and thoughts. But don't look for it with your eyes—it is hidden within your seeing. Don't listen for it with your ears—it is hidden within your hearing. Don't try to understand it, as it cannot be captured by thoughts nor expressed by words.

Just be still and quiet, it will emerge by itself,
all encompassing awareness—I AM.

we are made

to fly above the world

finer that a breath

lighter than a thought.

pure being

in illusion caught.

About the Author

As a child growing up in Romania, I was captivated by a popular children's story about a penguin named "Apolodor" who lived in Labrador. While this innocent little story made me dream of the rugged Canadian wilderness, I never imagined that my father (a geologist) would relocate our family to Newfoundland and Labrador during my teens. The Canadian culture, not to mention the intoxicating and pristine land, opened me to new ideas that were utterly unknown to my life in Romania.

During this time, I stumbled across a dusty, old yoga book and felt an immediate, strong connection. I diligently taught myself the postures while following the book's focus on fitness and flexibility. However, I soon realized that those strange exercises were opening me to something unexpected—something beyond the mere physical. As I learned more about the philosophy behind yoga, I became mesmerized by the incredible stories of Indian yogis, with their mystical powers and their outlandish ideas of life and rebirth that made more sense than anything I had ever heard.

It's been nearly thirty years later, and I still continue my self-directed yoga practice. During the past ten years or so, this has included meditation, which has played a paramount role in my adult life. By silencing the 'monkey mind,' I have learned to access spaces that are free from self-identification. There, I can feel, and sometimes glean knowledge from what appears to be an inexhaustible ocean of intuitive inspiration that feels 'true.'

As more insights started arriving from these spaces, I decided to scribble them on paper, in a manner akin to a dream journal. My musings eventually took the form of poems, which, thanks to the encouragement of friends and family, I am sharing with you now, even though I sometimes feel I'm more like their conduit rather than their author.

I sincerely hope my Butterfly Flutters make you feel as light-hearted and inspired as I felt when they arrived to me.